Naked Friends

Justin Grimbol

Also by Justin Grimbol

Hard Bodies

Drinking Until Morning

The Party Lords

The Creek

The Crud Masters

NAKED

FRIENDS

THIS BOOK IS DEDICATED TO BUTTS!
ALL THE BUTTS!

PART

ONE

1

A man walked into The Grimy Diner and sat at the counter. He was a big man with beady eyes.

"May I take your order, sir?" the waiter asked.

He was new and he was very nervous.

The large man just stared at him, suspiciously.

"He wants a meatloaf," Rosy, the owner, called out from the kitchen. "He always gets a meatloaf."

Rosy walked up to the counter, put her arm around the young, studly waiter's shoulder, and smiled.

"This pleasantly plump customer is Kevin, but we all call him Boner."

"That's not true," Boner said, blushing. "Nobody calls me that."

"It is true," she said. "It's the most true thing you have ever known."

The waiter laughed. His dimples were intense. He was so handsome. Where did Rosy find these kids? How did she convince them to work at The Grimy Diner? He should be a lifeguard, somewhere that's warm all the time. He should be rescuing skinny chicks in thongs. His smile was magic. Boner expected doves to fly out from behind him. He expected light to shoot out of the boy's eyes and fill the world with love.

"Do you want anything to drink?" the boy asked.

"Diet Pepsi please."

"Boner!" Rosy said. "You know we don't got Pepsi. I carry Coke products and Coke products only."

"I just keep hoping you'll get Pepsi one day. I love Pepsi."

"Don't talk in that baby voice," she said. "It makes you sound retarded."

Boner put his hand out. "So what's your name?" he asked.

The new waiter examined the big man's sweaty paw. He took a breath and shook it.

"I'm Steve," he said.

"Nice to meet you."

2

Rosy put the plate of meatloaf in front of Boner and watched him eat. Boner loved the meatloaf. He hated everything else Rosy cooked, but he loved her meatloaf. It was always slightly burnt, filled with onion bits, and wrapped in bacon. It was delicious. When he was finished, she brought him a beer. Every day he got one beer on the house.

"Your Grandma called," Rosy said.

"Yeah . . . "

"She wanted to know how you're doing."

"I'm doing great."

Rosy reached over and rubbed his bald head.

Boner appreciated Rosy's affection. Even when she was teasing him and grabbing on his man boobs, it felt kind.

"I'm a man now," he said. "I'm a grown up man. She's just upset that I am doing grown up things. She wants me to be a kid for eternity."

"You still living in your minivan?"

"Yeah! So? It's awesome! I park it in Mash Potato Park. Right next to the creek. I have a swing set like twenty feet away. It's awesome."

Rosy shook her head.

"It's called Mashashmanuek Park. It's an Indian name."

"I know. But I like to call it Mash Potato Park, 'cause mashed potatoes are awesome."

A waiter dropped a fork on the ground. He picked it up and gave it to the customer. The customer looked mortified, but didn't say anything. The woman just smiled nervously at the studly young waiter and wiped the fork with her napkin. Rosy saw all of this and laughed.

"God damn, that kid is stoned."

"They're all stoned," Boner said. "That's what makes them so friendly."

3

Boner's minivan was not an ordinary minivan. Three years earlier he had gotten it on a show called *Swag Mobile*, where a has-been rapper took junky looking cars and made them fancy and futuristic looking. The guy really went to town on the thing. He took out the back seats and put in a hot tub. The back window doubled as a movie screen. It had more computer panels than a spaceship. The outside looked like a carnival ride. Boner told them he liked metal so, keeping that in mind, the rapper and his crew painted it black. The rims were holographic skulls. On the side was a painting of naked warrior women fighting. It was rad.

Since then, Boner had gotten out of the metal phase. But he still appreciated how rad his van looked. It looked intimidating and—he was sure—it kept thieves away.

He hadn't used the hot tub in a while. Well, he hadn't been using it as a tub. Since he had left home, he had used it as a bed. It was filled with pillows and blankets.

His little minivan home was very comfortable, but that night he felt homesick. He wandered around the parking lot. He sat on a swing. He listened to the creek.

The sky was starless. It started to rain and he retreated into the minivan. He curled up in his hot tub bed.

Just before he dozed off, another vehicle pulled into the parking lot. Boner could hear the bass rumbling. And then he heard girls laughing. They sounded drunk. It was impossible to sleep. He turned on a movie and that distracted him for an hour before the battery ran out. The minivan felt stuffy. He started sweating.

The sun rose.

Finally the car full of laughing girls drove away. Sometime around six a.m. he was able to drift off into a decent sleep.

4

Old man Boli knocked on the minivan's window. The backdoor made a robot noise as it opened. Boner crawled out. He smelled like crotch sweat. It was eight a.m. That meant he had only slept for a couple of hours.

"You know you're not supposed to sleep here," the old man said.

"I know. But you love me."

"I don't love you. I dated your grandma once. That's all."

"You love me just a little," Boner said.

"No. Not even a little."

"I love you a little."

The old man shook his head.

Boner laughed. "Old men are so grumpy."

"You wanna smoke?" the old man asked.

"No, it makes me lightheaded."

"I thought you kids like that sort of thing."

The old man lit up a cigarette. They sat on the minivan's bumper. Boli smoked.

Boner told him about the people partying the night before.

"That's normal," the old man said. "What's not normal is you sleeping in this weird looking minivan."

"I think you secretly like that I live here."

The old man shook his head and put out his cigarette. He walked to his lawn mower and started cutting the grass. He was the best lawn mower in town. Boner was sure of that. The park grass looked tamed. Like it wouldn't bother growing even if old man Boli let it. The town also put him in charge of mowing the graveyard and the lawn surrounding Town Hall. But Mash Potato Park was his pride and joy. It was obvious.

Boner thought about going back to bed, but it was too hot and stuffy in there. Instead, he walked over to the gas station around the corner and bought a Sunkist and a bag of peanut M&M's for breakfast. He also bought a balsa wood plane.

A kid walked up to him. He was little and curious.

"You want to have a contest?" Boner asked. "We can see whose plane can go the farthest."

The kid nodded.

Boner went first. He tossed his plane. It flew up, did a loop-di-loop, and then flew into the woods, hiding itself.

The kid was excited to throw his.

"Watch this!" the kid yelled.

He tossed his plane. It went up and then dived down quickly and crashed into the ground.

Boner laughed. "You so lost. My plane kicked your plane's ass."

The kid looked upset. His mother walked up to him and looked at Boner.

"Hi, my name's Boner," he said, holding out his hand.

The mother did not shake his hand. She rushed her child away.

Boner wished he had told her his real name.

5

Old man Boli helped jumpstart Boner's minivan. Boner spent the rest of the day basking in the air conditioning, watching movies. He left his minivan once, to get a meatloaf at The Grimy.

After he ate, he went back in his minivan and set his windows to extra dark, so nobody could see in. He got on the internet and looked up some porn. He wished he could use his computer while chilling in his hot tub. But that wasn't possible. His computer screen came out of the front passenger side dashboard. The keyboard folded out of the middle console. It was not a comfortable way to masturbate.

After he spanked it, he checked his email. There was an email from someone named Jake Reed. Jake was requesting his services as a private detective.

Boner was confused. He wasn't a private detective. Boner scanned down through the message. Jake Reed mentioned an ad on craigslist. Boner remembered he *had* put an ad up saying he was a

20

private detective, but this was years ago. Rosy from The Grimy had convinced him you can't just decide to be a private detective. Boner had posted lots of silly stuff on craigslist. He had posted an ad saying he was a video game specialist. If your kid was having trouble beating a video game he would beat it for them. He once posted an ad saying he was a master chef. He even tried to start his own cab service. He got a few calls. But no one wanted to sit in a hot tub filled with pillows. He had posted that he was a massage therapist specializing in butt massages. He had posted a lot of things. Usually people didn't respond. And when they did, it usually didn't take them long to realize he wasn't a professional. But here he had a guy emailing him offering to pay him five hundred dollars up front to help him with a case. Five hundred dollars was a lot of dollars for a man living in his minivan.

He wrote back and told Jake he would take the case. Jake emailed back immediately. They made plans to meet at The Grimy the next morning.

Boner felt pride surge through his system. He was no longer unemployed. He was a private detective. It was a fine job. A damn fine job.

6

"Listen Rosy, I'm a professional now. So no calling me Boner. No grabbing my boobs. No rubbing my bald head for good luck. This guy is coming here to talk about business."

"Your head is extra shiny today. I feel like I can see the future in it."

"I showered. Twice. Okay, three times. I'm really clean right now. Stop staring at my head."

"And I like the suit."

"My grandma bought it for me. She was really excited about my new job. I am going to wear it every day. It's my detective uniform."

"You might want to wash it occasionally."

A young man walked into The Grimy Diner. He looked nervous. Confused. Paranoid. He told Rosy his name was Jake and that he was supposed to meet someone there. Boner stood up, walked over, and shook his hand.

"Hi! I'm Boner. And I'm a private detective."

It took him a moment to realize he just gave out his nickname and not his real name. He blushed hard. But Jake didn't seem fazed.

They sat down. Jake looked like a gym teacher. He had a crew cut, muscular arms, his t-shirt was tucked into his shorts, and he had that intense look in his eyes Boner figured came from too much exercising.

"All the waiters here are young and male and very attractive," Jake said. "Are they prostitutes?"

"I don't think so," Boner said.

"If they were they could make a pretty penny. They're all very attractive."

"Sure. I guess."

Rosy handed Jake a menu. He looked it over carefully and ordered a grilled cheese sandwich, "ungrilled."

"So you just want a cheese sandwich?"

"Yes please."

7

"Okay, here's the deal," Jake said. "I'm a quiet guy. I keep to myself. I moved here a year ago. I'm from a little town in northern Oregon called Astoria. This place reminds me of Astoria, actually. It's quiet. It looks like nothing's been updated since the late '80s. And people are nice. They don't act nice. But they are. You can just tell. All I want to do is fit in. Make a nice, discreet life for myself here. That's all. But somehow I have been caught up in some bad shit."

"Like what?"

Rosy stood over them. She looked very intrigued.

"Do you mind?" Boner said. "This is very private."

Rosy winked at him and walked away.

Boner asked Jake to continue.

"Last night I was walking home from the new Rocky movie . . ."

"*Rocky Vs. Rambo*? How was it?"

"It was profound. It was . . . life changing. The film is very intellectual."

"Ah, I knew it would be."

"I was in a great mood. All I wanted to do was walk around and think about the movie I had just seen. But these two goons started following me around. I tried to lose them but they were really on me. At one point I heard them talking about wanting to kick my ass. They said they were going to rape me and then break my ribs."

Boner's eyes widened. "They were rapists?"

"Definitely."

Boner was confused. Jake did not look like the kind of guy people would want to rape. But then he thought of all the weird fetishes out there. Maybe people had a weird musclebound nerd fetish. Or a gym teacher fetish. Or a buzz cut fetish. Who knew? Anything was possible.

"Why did they want to rape you so badly?"

"I think someone sent them after me."

"Who?"

"I don't know. That is what I need you to figure out."

"Me?"

"Yes. I have a feeling the following people will have an idea of what's going on."

Jake passed him a piece of paper.

"Why do you think these people can help me out?"

"'Cause they're sketchy. I'm usually very picky about who I associate myself with. But these people got under my radar. Do you think you can take on the case?"

"Sure."

Jake passed him an envelope filled with money.

"This is awesome," Boner said. "I mean, I get money like this all the time. 'Cause I'm a detective."

Rosy brought Jake his cheese sandwich. He took a bite out of it. He looked at the sandwich thoughtfully.

"This is really good," he said.

"I like the meatloaf," said Boner.

Jake chewed slowly. He looked like he wanted to moan but held it in.

"How did you escape the rapists?" Boner asked.

Jake lifted his leg. His calf was gigantic. Muscular.

"I'm really fast."

"That's awesome," Boner said. "I don't really run much. I have a minivan."

"I like that. Minivans are discreet. You will need to be discreet."

Boner didn't know what 'discreet' meant.

"Oh its super discreet. It's discreet as hell. It has holographic skulls on the tires and naked warrior chicks painted on it."

There was a long, awkward silence.

"Are you sure you can handle this case?" Jake asked.

Boner rolled his eyes in an attempt to seem overly confident. "Obviously. Don't worry. I'm good at this. Rapists are terrified of me. It's a fact."

8

Boner sat in the passenger seat of his minivan. He pressed a code onto the control panel on the armrest. A computer screen lifted out of the dashboard. The keyboard popped out and pushed into his gut. He logged onto Facebook. He had a friend request from Jake Reed. He looked over his profile. He had already befriended everyone at The Grimy Diner. Including the waiters. He only had one profile pic—a photo of Rocky Balboa. He had a few pics he was tagged in. Boner clicked to enlarge them. Two of the pics weren't even of Jake. They were of action movie posters. The only real picture of him was small, like it was taken with an old cell phone. It was of him standing at the Grand Canyon, alone.

Jake's page was lonely. Boner wanted to get away from it. He looked over the list Jake had given him. There was the only name he recognized. Tyler. AKA The Scientist. The kid was nuts. He had known him all his life. When they were little he knew the best sex games. This kid could make a slumber party feel like a Roman orgy.

His nickname used to be The Inventor because he would invent so many awesome sex games. Like Strip Marco Polo, and Strip Duck Duck Goose, Strip Go Fish, and Butt Shark. Butt Shark was the most popular. The rules were simple. It was Tag, but you had to tag people with your naked butt. Usually Boner was made to be the shark. He knew this was an insult. They chose him because he had the nastiest butt. It was covered in pimples and slimy. But he loved being the Butt Shark. Everyone seemed so terrified. It made him feel powerful. He was good at it, too. One time he tagged this kid right on the forehead. The kid was underwater at the time. But he could hear him screaming. Other times they would choose a girl to be the shark. That was also a good time. All the other boys pretended to be scared of the female butt. This confused Boner. Why were they running away? They acted just as scared of girl butts as his own. But they were supposed to like girl butt. Girl butt was sun in the sky to boys that age. Boner was the only one that didn't fear the girl butt. He didn't really run from it. He pretended to, but that was all part of the act. He lured the butt like a matador. He tempted it. And then, when it headed for him, he ducked down and let it hit him in the face. The girl eventually caught on to what he was doing. Boner was banned from playing boy-girl Butt Shark. After awhile he was only allowed to play when it was just dudes and he was the shark.

Boner found Tyler's page. It seemed the boy had changed his nickname again. He was now 'The Doctor.' He had evolved from The Scientist and The Inventor to this, 'The Doctor.' It all made sense to Boner. Boner wished his nickname could evolve. He was so tired of being called Boner.

The Doctor had over a thousand pictures. Ninety-five percent of them were with girls. And he looked wild. He had a massive orange afro. His clothing was thuggy, like it had been in high school, but a bit more weirded-out. He had gold chains around his neck. At the end of the gold chain was a framed picture of his mother.

Boner scanned the pictures hoping to find a shot of him with Jake, but he couldn't find any. He scanned his friends list. Jake wasn't on there either.

The Doctor was a sexual deviant, so maybe he was one of the rapists. No, Boner had a hard time believing that. The Doctor was chill. He would cop a feel and even grab an ass, but he would never make anyone scream in pain. He would never torture someone like that.

Boner looked into his page. The kid listed his phone number and his address. He also listed all the girls he had ever boinked. Then there was a list of all the girls he ever dry humped. There were so many girls. It was way into the double digits, almost triple.

Boner didn't have a cell phone. But his van operated as a phone. He dialed the kid's number on the keypad. The Doctor's voice boomed over the speaker system.

"Who the fuck is this?"

"Hi Tyler. It's Boner. Are you okay? You sound out of breath."

"Holy shit. Fuck that. This is Boner?"

"You remember me?"

"Of course I do. Motherfucker, you were the Butt Shark Champion."

Boner giggled.

"I was pretty good at that."

"Motherfucker, you were an ass master blaster. Shit, you fucked up the whole world with that big ass ass of yours. You hit it like the asteroid that killed the dinosaurs."

"It's not that big."

"Dude, come over, we'll Butt Shark right now!"

"Seriously?"

"Motherfucker, I'm always serious. I'm like a college professor from the 1800s, I'm so serious."

It seemed unreal. Were they actually about to play Butt Shark? It had been years. His heart raced. He slid behind the wheel. He peeled out of the parking lot and headed toward The Doctor's place.

9

The Doctor still lived at his parents' house. They used to have an above ground pool. But things got wild during a party a bunch of years back. Too many people got in. The thing broke open, flooding the front yard.

Had they gotten a new one?

Boner drove up to the house. It was a nice little house, hidden under large pines. He looked around the perimeter. He couldn't find a pool anywhere. They weren't actually playing Butt Shark. The Doctor was lying. Why would he do that? Not that it mattered. Even if they were going to play Butt Shark, he wouldn't be allowed to join in. Maybe the ban had been lifted. It had been a long time. A damn long time. Maybe he was allowed to play Butt Shark with girls again. It didn't matter. They didn't have a pool.

Boner knocked on the door.

"Door's open!" he heard a female voice yell.

He walked in.

The Doctor rushed up to him and gave him a hug.

"Damn, you lookin' good. Have a seat you badass, curvy ass motherfucker!" The Doctor said.

Boner sat on a La-Z-Boy and leaned back. He looked around. The house looked the same as it did when they were young. Same furniture. Same massive flat screen.

"Where are your parents?" Boner asked.

"They don't live here anymore," The Doctor said. "Motherfuckers divorced. Mom's living in New Jersey with some dude running a tanning salon. Lady startin' to look leathery and creepy. Dad still hangs here sometimes, but dude handlin' business. They got him working at corporate headquarters in Rochester. So, for all intents and purposes, this shit is my shit."

"That's so cool."

"It's leisurely as hell. I'm not even dealing with landlords and all that shit, ya hear."

The girls were looking at Boner suspiciously. There were four of them. One was super short. She had cornrows and mean, icy eyes. She sat with her legs crisscrossed on the coffee table. Then there was a girl Boner had met before. She was sitting on the armrest of the couch. People called her Rhino Booty. It was meant as an insult, but Boner thought girls with rhino booties were the best.

There was a fourth girl. Boner didn't recognize her. She didn't look as suspicious as the other girls. He tried to get out of the La-Z-Boy, but he had trouble leaning forward. Finally he heaved forward and nearly fell on the girl.

"I'm Boner," he said.

"I'm Clitty. I just moved here."

"Clitty? What's a clitty?"

"You're shitting me, right?"

The Doctor laughed hysterically. "What's a clitty? How funny is this motherfucker? For real, I'm glad you here dude. You a wild dude. You humpty dumpty John Candy bald eagle motherfucker."

"No, really, what's a clitty?"

The girls shook their heads. They groaned. They rolled their eyes. They showed their dismay in every way possible. How could this guy not know what a clitty was?

"You need to look that shit up on Wikipedia," The Doctor said. "That shit makes chicks feel good. You rub on that shit. Clitty got a big one. She comes hard as fuck, too. Straight up comes hard, bro. Comes and holds onto the bed post like there's a hole in the spaceship and she's being sucked into outer space."

Clitty punched his arm. "Will you shut up?"

"So why do people call you Boner?" Tiny asked.

"I don't know," Boner said.

"Yes you do," The Doctor said. "This wild animal got more Boner's than anyone I know. Kid had a boner all the time when we were just little bitty motherfuckers. He constantly had boner blazing. It got to the point where his Grandma wouldn't allow him to wear sweat pants or anything that made that nasty ass boner too obvious. Dude was tenting hard. Motherfucker!"

Boner looked grumpy.

"I hated that. I thought that was so stupid. I couldn't understand why people were so grossed out by my boner. Everybody gets them."

"I don't get them," Rhino Booty said.

"I know. I mean all us guys get boners. And girls like boners. So I didn't understand why getting a boner couldn't be cool."

"I was cool," The Doctor said. "Everyone sit down. I got tales to tell about a boy named Boner."

The Doctor was surprisingly nostalgic. He loved to talk about the past. He told the girls a bunch of stories about Boner. He told them about the time he ate a whole pizza pie. He told them about Butt Shark. About the epic games of truth or dare they had played. How he once sucked a titty for an hour. With the bra on. The girls loved that one. The Doctor had an endless supply of tales. He told them about the time Boner fell asleep during class so deeply he got up, took off his pants, and pissed on the floor. "It was a great dream," Boner said. "I thought I was a volcano. But then I woke up and I was in so much trouble."

The girls laughed. It felt nice to make girls laugh.

The Doctor snuck off to his room and came back with a Super Soaker 500. It was one of those new, futuristic looking Super Soakers. It was not the kind they grew up with. The gun wasn't as big as many other Super Soakers, but it looked mean. It was the thuggiest of the Super Soakers. The Doctor walked up to one of the girls and stuck it in her mouth. She sucked on it and he shot it into her mouth. She must really love staying hydrated, Boner thought.

He gave each girl a little Super Soaker action. Then he shot it into his own mouth.

"You want some?" he asked Boner.

"No, I'll just use a glass to drink my water."

He laughed. "This ain't water. Shit. This is the real shit. This is filled with whiskey, motherfucker."

"Really?"

"Real as shit. Nothing gets more real than Super Soaker filled with whiskey."

He took the Super Soaker in the mouth. The whiskey was strong. Tasted ugly. Made his gums burn.

"That was so good," he said.

"I know. You love this shit."

They got drunk. The girls loosened up. They became talkative. They loved teasing The Doctor. They loved to make fun of his sexual performance.

"The Doctor over here loves to just lie there and let me do all the work," Clitty yelled. "He acts like a quadriplegic when we're fucking."

"You know why we call him The Doctor," the little one said. Her name was Debby. "'Cause he got this pointy dick. We call it the scalpel."

The Doctor laughed. "Don't listen to them, Boner. These girls are nuts. They forgetful. They got Alzheimer's or something. They call me The Doctor 'cause this thing saves lives, motherfucker."

He stood on the couch and grabbed his dick. The girls laughed. One flicked her tongue at him like a snake.

Rhino Booty rolled her eyes. "I swear he knows where the clit and the G spot is," she said. "But he avoids it like the plague. I sit on his face and he licks everything but the clit."

The Doctor loved this. He acted like they were complimenting him. "You all love my shit. You can't get enough of this shit. This shit is the shit!"

Clitty sat next to Boner on the armrest and leaned against him.

"You're comfy," she said.

"Thanks."

She leaned even closer. Soon she was using him as a chair. They weren't snuggling. She was just sitting on him, enjoying the fleshy cushioning. Boner didn't mind.

"The Doctor's so skinny," Rhino Booty said. "But his dick smells like a fat guy's dick. It's so pungent and swampy. It's like bayou down there."

"That's my pheromones and shit," The Doctor said. "Y'all don't realize it, but that dick stank has put a spell on all y'all. My dick's like Harry Potter's wand. It's magical and shit. But it don't work unless it stink a little. It gotta stink. I mean, it gotta stink. That stink good. My ball stink will rule the world. My crotch stink so good, yo! My crotch make Santa's reindeer fly and shit, y'all! Motherfuck-er!"

"Excuse me . . . " Boner said to Clitty.

She either didn't hear him or was ignoring him.

"Rhino, tell that story about the time you and that one dude did that weird thing," Clitty said.

"Oh, you mean the dude with the big dick?"

"Yes. That one."

"Well, The Doctor over here got really into watching us with other dudes. So he brought over this guy, this really old gnarly guy. And the dude had the biggest dick. We were tired of the scalpel, so we went to town on that crazy whale dick. And I was riding the dick and The Doctor starts licking my asshole."

"You licked her butthole?" Boner asked.

"Hell yeah."

"That's weird," Boner said. "Isn't it pooey down there?"

Clitty elbowed him. "Don't be rude. Rhino got the cleanest asshole in the world. I've licked that thing plenty of times."

Boner giggled.

"So anyway . . ." Rhino continued. "I was riding the big dick and the old dude gave me this weird look. I asked him what was up. He whispered to me that The Doctor over here was licking on his nut sack."

The girls laughed wildly.

"But that's not weird," Boner said.

"What the eff?" Tiny said. "You don't think it's weird that The Doctor licked a ball sack."

The Doctor gave him a confused smiled. He couldn't wait to hear what Boner had to say about ball sacks.

"Well, it's weird. But people lick balls. They do it all the time. Butthole licking, that's what's weird."

The girls were shocked.

"You're shitting me," Clitty said.

"You never done that?" Tiny asked.

"You never licked a butt?" Rhino repeated.

"I've never licked a butt."

"Fuck you!" Rhino said.

"What is this, the '90s?" Clitty said. "Who doesn't eat ass nowadays? I'd lick my own butt if I could."

Clitty and Tiny high-fived.

Boner started giggling. "You girls are gross."

Clitty didn't like that. She got pissed off. Tiny stopped dancing.

She turned the music off.

"Tiny, show him the morningstar," Clitty said.

Tiny and Rhino moved the coffee table up to Boner. Boner looked confused. He didn't understand what was going on. He looked to The Doctor for help. The Doctor shrugged his shoulders.

Tiny got up on the table. She pulled her pink leggings down. Boner's eyes widened. Of all the asses there, hers was the one he was least curious about. Still, he liked it. It was tiny, like the rest of her. It was tiny, but it had character.

She bent over. He could see her butthole. She spread her cheeks even wider. So much butthole. He liked it. It was ugly. There was so much rough, wrinkly skin.

"Lick it," Clitty said.

"What?"

"Lick it!" the girls chanted. "LICK IT! LICK IT! LICK IT!"

"Ummm."

Boner got nervous.

The Doctor raised a squirt gun up to Boner's temple. "Lick it," he said. "Or I'll shoot."

Boner laughed nervously. "But that thing's filled with whisky."

"Nope. I switched it when you weren't looking. I filled it with skin-eating acid. If you don't eat that poor girl's little butthole, I'm going to spray you down with this acid and make your dumb ass look like Two Face."

Boner looked at him. Was that possible? He seemed serious. It was scary.

The girls kept chanting.

"LICK IT! LICK IT! LICK IT!"

Boner closed his eyes and stuck out his tongue. He slowly moved his face toward the butt. He could smell it. The smell wasn't nasty, like the way poop's nasty. But it wasn't a clean smell either.

The chanting intensified.

"LICK IT! LICK IT! LICK IT!"

Finally the tip of his tongue touched the girl's sphincter.

It wasn't so bad.

He thought he was done, then Rhino grabbed his head and pushed it into open ass crack.

His face slammed against her butt.

It was warm. And surprisingly pleasant.

He fell back and looked at the girls. They were all laughing and dancing around. The music was back on.

Their dancing got crazier. It didn't look like dancing at all. They were jumping on things and wrestling and whipping their butts and boobs out. The Doctor was dancing with them.

Boner didn't know how to act. He just sat on the La-Z-Boy, thinking about Tiny's butt and how warm it felt.

"That was awesome," he said to himself.

Clitty heard him and laughed. She came over and smelled his cheek. She pretended it smelled gross. She waved her hands in front of her nose as if shooing away a poopy odor. But he could tell she was pretending. There was a faint odor and it wasn't pleasant. But he liked it. He could tell she liked it too.

"I want more butt!" he yelled.

They all applauded.

"He's hooked!" The Doctor said.

He was drunk and feeling brave.

"I said I want more butt!"

Clitty unbuttoned her jeans and pulled them down. Her butt was pale and had a little acne. Boner grabbed her waist and shoved his face in. It wasn't as warm. Her ass cheeks were clenched together. He couldn't get in far enough.

"MORE!" he yelled.

They laughed but refused to give him more ass.

The Doctor gave him a hug. "It's over, bro. That's the most ass you going to get this evening."

"But I want more," Boner said.

"I know you do. I know you do."

Boner danced with the girls. He saw The Doctor slip away into a back room. He had forgotten the mission at hand. He had to talk to The Doctor and find out what he knew about Jake and the rapists. He danced with the girls for a while longer. The girls found it funny at first. Then they got annoyed.

"Okay," Tiny said. "Stop, you're just acting like an ass now."

Boner got self-conscious and went into the back room to find The Doctor.

10

The Doctor stood in the kitchen eating cereal.

"I needed a cereal break," he said. "Those girls are tiring. They tire me out, for real. I needed a treat. The Doctor needs his treats."

Boner walked up to The Doctor. They embraced.

"Were you really going to spray acid on me?" he asked.

"Naw, that thing was empty. You actually believed that shit? You crazy. Where the fuck would I find skin-eating acid? Shit . . . "

Boner laughed. "I got to tell you a secret."

"What?"

"I'm a private investigator now."

"No way. That's wild as hell. You narc me out to any cops I'll beat your fat ass, you better believe that."

"I would never turn you in. I just need to know if you know this kid named Jake?"

"Jake Williams? Little Dick Jake?"

"No, this kid has a buzz cut and I think his last name is Reed."

"I don't know, man. What does he look like again?"

"Like a gym teacher. But kinda nerdy."

"Oh shit, you're talking about that dude. Oh fuck, yeah, I know him. Let me tell you a story about that nerd. He got really drunk in the Headlights one night. I mean fucked up. He was all over this bartender. Poor bitch. Couldn't stand the nerd. She was hating her job that night, man. Fuck. It was sad to watch. I bought the kid a drink. Nice enough dude. Then he sent me a thank you letter. No shit. A thank you letter. And at first I was like, shit, I guess that's chill. I mean, I'm a pretty great guy. I'm motherfuckin' exceptional as fuck. Then he sent me another letter. This one was just sorta rambling, like a text. So I saw him and I was like, yo, just text me, here's my number and shit. But he texted me nonstop, so I had to block his number."

"Do you know anyone who might want to rape him?" Boner asked.

"What the fuck? No. Who even asks that?"

Boner pulled out the list of leads Jake had given him.

"This is hard. Being a detective is confusing. You know anyone on this list?"

The Doctor took the sweaty piece of paper and looked it over.

"Yeah, this chick is kinda weird. You should look her up on Facebook. Her pics are nuts."

"I tried, but I couldn't find her."

"That's 'cause the girly don't use her real name. She goes by Lady Moonbeam or some shit."

Boner wrote the name on the list. He felt very professional.

"Do you have a laptop?" he asked The Doctor.

"Shit, I got all sorts of technology, motherfucker. I got mad gadgets."

The Doctor led him to his room. Pictures from porn mags from the '90s covered his walls. His bed was massive. It looked like two queens pressed together. It smelled like ball sack. The Doctor reached under the covers and pulled out an old HP. He handed it to Boner.

"If you want to get the internet you have to sit here," he said. He pointed to the center of the bed. "That's the only place we get it."

Boner got on the bed and found the signal. He logged onto Facebook. He looked up Lady Moonbeam. Was this her? The girl in the pictures was wearing elf ears and not much clothing. He had never seen a girl look so nerdy and sexy at the same time. There were a bunch of pics of her in a bathing suit playing with swords. Her body was pale and sloppy. But sloppy in a sexy way.

Looking at the pics gave Boner a boner. He looked through the pics. One of was of her butt with her bathing suit wedged in the crack and cellulite somehow making it look more sexy and more jiggly. He couldn't stop staring at her. He wished there were more pics.

He went onto YouTube and looked up "nerds naked." There were a few videos, but none of the girls looked as good as Moonbeam. Then he looked up "Moonbeam." He found a video of her in a bathing suit fighting another nerd, a male nerd, with a foam sword.

Boner reached down his pants and played with his horny parts. It was sweaty down there. And he liked that. But he was pretty sure most girls would find it to be nasty.

"Wake the fuck up!" he heard The Doctor yell.

Boner closed the laptop and walked to the living room.

At this point, the girls had fallen asleep. The Doctor was compulsively taking bong hits. Boner joined him.

"They are so sleepy," The Doctor yelled. "It makes me so sad. I'm sad as a motherfucker."

The Doctor didn't fall asleep. He just smoked and stared off, looking catatonic. Maybe he's sleeping with his eyes open? Boner thought.

Boner got up and went to the kitchen. The refrigerator was well stocked. He started making omelets. The smell woke everyone up. They stumbled into the kitchen and ate a feast.

11

The rain poured then stopped abruptly. Sunlight came out for a moment. Beams of light shot out of the clouds like pictures from a church bulletin. Then the clouds darkened and poured again.

Boner hid in his minivan. He was surprised he couldn't sleep. Usually he could sleep all day if he wanted. He had actually been busy, investigating, doing detective shit, drinking, licking butts, cooking eggs, more detective shit, and still he couldn't sleep. His mind raced, going over what little clues he had gathered.

He watched a bunch of detective movies as research. *Dick Tracy. Who Framed Roger Rabbit? Fargo. Fletch,* etc.

Eventually, around four p.m., he drifted to sleep. But his car phone woke him. It rang as loud as an old pay phone. He tried to ignore it. The ringing stopped. A moment passed. There was a loud beep, indicating he had a message. He tried to go back to sleep. He couldn't.

He awoke and checked his messages. Jake's voice boomed over

the minivan's speakers. He was wondering if Boner had made any progress on the case. Boner called him back and assured him the case was moving along.

Boner looked out the window. Old Man Boli was on his mower. He was maneuvering around playground equipment. It was loud but calming. Boner took some Benadryl and waited to pass out.

12

For Boner, Facebook was a delicate art. You had to be patient and graceful. It was important to always have a cupcake nearby in case things got tense. Cupcakes calmed him down. It was important to stay calm, especially when stalking a girl he liked or, in this case, a girl he was sorta being paid to stalk.

On the first day, Boner made sure to like a bunch of her Facebook posts. He figured that would get her vaguely familiar with him. On the second day, he wrote her his first comment. She had posted pictures of herself eating cheesecake. Hell, Boner couldn't help but write something. "Dear God, I would do anything for a cheesecake right now. Literally, anything."

She wrote back: "lol. Omg. I know. Cheese cake is God."

Boner wrote: "Oh my God, I hope God's a cheese cake. And then when you eat him he just comes back to life. That would be awesome."

She wrote: "You're funny."

That got him excited.

On the fourth day he posted a picture of a sexy elf chick on her page. She loved it.

That night they chatted.

Moonbeam: "You into EW?"

BONER: "What's that?"

Moonbeam: "Elf Wars."

BONER: "Sounds cool."

Moonbeam: "It is. You like fantasy?"

BONER: "Elves are cool. I used to want to be one of Santa's helpers when I was young."

Moonbeam: "You're silly."

That was it. Simple. Sweet.

On the fifth day she sent him a message, inviting him to play some D&D with her and her friends. He had to look up what D&D was. He found a Wikipedia page on Dungeons and Dragons.

Holy shit, this sounds like so much fun, he thought.

13

"Boner!"

He turned around and saw a girl running toward him. It was Clitty. She had just come out of Conca's Pizza. She looked rowdy. Her top barely covered her tiny tits. The oversized sweatshirt hung like a cape. And her leggings were so tight they seemed to be see-through. Her bleach blond hair was fancy. She had put it up in big curls that looked like waves of light.

"Hi," Boner said.

She pushed him.

"Act more excited to see me, you dumb oaf."

"Sorry."

"What are you, embarrassed 'cause you got all anal obsessed last night? Stop being a pussy! A man that can't flirt when he's sober and in public isn't worth a shit to me."

He smiled and blushed.

"What are you doing?"

"Going to go play D&D."

"No shit. My brother used to play that. He and his dork friends used to play that shit for hours. It looked fun. They let me play once. I was this sexy troll. I was badass. Then I hooked up with one of them. I was like eleven and my brother's friend was like sixteen, so it was a big deal. They stopped playing D&D at my place after that. I think my brother is still mad at me about that shit."

"I've never played it. Is it hard?"

"You're shitting me. You never played this shit? I figured you were a full-blown nerd."

"Nope. Only part nerd. Part something else."

She laughed. "You eat too much butt to be a nerd now."

Boner smiled. He liked that idea. Ass cures all nerdiness. Who would have known?

"I have to go," Boner said, trying to sound as polite as possible. "I'm late."

"Cool, I'll come with."

"But you're not invited."

"I just invited myself."

They walked down Main Street, out of town, past the old watch factory.

"Where's your vehicle?" Clitty asked.

"I thought we could walk."

"Walking is so '90s."

He couldn't tell if that was an insult or a compliment.

14

A weeping willow stood in front of Moonbeam's house. It was
sunny. It was the warmest day of spring they had so far. Clitty ran
under the weeping willow and played with its vines. The house was
run down, but cozy looking. The inside was furnished with an-
tiques. Moonbeam's bedroom was on the second floor. It was
small and packed with nerds.

Moonbeam was annoyed. She didn't want Clitty there. She was
not invited. Most of the gamers were male and Clitty made them
nervous.

Moonbeam told her she could watch but it would be too complicated to give her a character.

"C'mon, put me in coach."

One of the larger nerds felt bad for her. He was the dungeon
master. He did not think it would be that hard to create a character
sheet for her.

"I guess we can add another character," she said. "What do you wanna be?"

"I just want to be sexy and wear a chain-mail bikini and ride a horse!" Clitty said.

"I guess you can be that," Moonbeam said.

"Boner, what are you going to be?"

"The Terminator."

There was a long moment of silence. The nerds were dumbfounded.

"The what?"

"The Terminator."

"Fuck yeah!" Clitty said. "That's badass."

"But the Terminator is a robot," Moonbeam said.

"I know. From the future."

Boner had one of his doofy little chubby cheeked smiles. It was the type of smile you usually saw on babies, not grown men. It made people want to talk to him very gently.

"Here's the thing," Moonbeam said. "This game we are playing takes place in the distant past, not the future."

"But the Terminator time travels. So, if you think about it, it makes complete sense that he would be in the past."

A lanky nerd nodded his head. "His logic is sound."

"Fine. Whatever. Be a Terminator."

Clitty high-fived Boner.

"Let's start the mission," Moonbeam said.

The dungeon master explained to them that they were all meeting in a pub. He took great time going over the details, how the dwarven bartender looked, how lizard man in the cloak kept staring at them.

"Finally the lizard man comes over. He says he has a quest for you. Do you accept?"

"We do," Moonbeam said.

Boner raised his hand.

"Yes, T-100, what is your move?"

"I kick out the bench from under him and then I lift my shotgun to his face and I yell, 'Where is John Conner!'"

Clitty laughed.

The nerds looked confused.

"The lizard refused to answer such a ridiculous question."

"Then I shoot him in the face."

The dungeon master had him roll some weird looking dice. Boner was confused. It all seemed too complicated. It was like math class times ten or something.

"The lizard is dead. Quest over."

"Are you serious?" Moonbeam yelled.

The nerds looked bummed out. Moonbeam looked like she was about to cry. Boner regretted shooting the lizard man, even though he was sure that's what the Terminator would do in that situation. Still, the nerds were upset. They liked the lizard guy for some reason. They wanted to go on his quest. They were sad he was dead.

"You ruined the game," the chunky Dungeon Master said.

The kid was fat, like Boner, but his fat seemed slimier, like it was about to melt into liquid form and seep into the carpet.

"I'm sorry," Boner said.

Clitty didn't like how sad Boner was.

"Don't get all up in Boner's face like that, nerd. Motherfucker. Seriously, dude was just playing your dumb ass game. He didn't break any rules."

"We told him he should pick another character, now the quest is ruined."

"Fuck your quest, Jabba the Hut-looking motherfucker. Put a new shirt on. That one barely fits. You need a muumuu. Fuck this. We don't need your shit. We're out."

Clitty stood up. She grabbed Boner's hand and led him to the door.

"Fuck you nerds."

Before he left, Boner asked Moonbeam for her number.

"I don't have a cell phone," she said.

Clitty laughed. "Who doesn't own a cell phone."

"I don't. My parents think they give people cancer. Like microwaves."

"Microwaves give people cancer?" Boner said.

"I need to get back to my friends. So . . . later."

"Thanks for inviting me," he said.

"Whatever."

Boner and Clitty ran outside. They headed down the road, past the old historic fire station, to a bridge that went over the creek. The water was high from all the rain they had been getting. What was usually a calm swimming hole was a raging rapid.

"What the fuck just happened?" Clitty said.

"I was just role playing," Boner said.

Boner felt bad. He had ruined their game.

"Did you smell that one nerd?" Clitty said.

Boner nodded. "He smelled like awful."

That whole experience had felt strange and dirty. Plus he felt unprofessional. He was supposed to get information out of Moonbeam, not annoy her and ruin her night. Now he didn't know if she was ever going to talk to him again.

He felt like he had to do something to make up for it, something to help the case.

"Maybe we should just walk around until we find people that look like rapists," Boner said.

"What?" Clitty keeled over laughing. "That's the worst idea I've ever heard."

She leaned into Boner as she laughed. Boner put his hand on her back.

"I'm serious. I gotta find out who's trying to rape my friend."

"I think there are better ways to find that shit out."

Clitty's cell phone rang.

"Shit, it's The Doctor. I told him I would help him with his website tonight. He gets so grumpy sometimes."

"He has a website?"

"Buttsharkuniversity.blogspot.com," she said. "It's super lame and he sucks at the internet, so I always have to help him. If I don't he has a hissy fit."

She kissed him on the cheek and ran off.

Boner stood there and listened to the water run under the bridge.

15

Boner sat in The Grimy Diner playing Battleship with one of the waiters. The kid's name was Garth. He was scrappy looking and laughed a lot. Boner liked him a lot.

"Are you serious right now?" Rosy said.

"He sunk all my ships," Boner said. "But I have one little ship left and he can't find it."

"This game is so intense," Garth said, unable to look away from the board.

"It's one thing to be lazy," Rosy said. "But to play a board game at work brings laziness to a whole new level."

"There's no customers," he said.

Rosy pointed to a man sitting at the corner table. It was obvious he was starving, dizzy with hunger, and had been waiting for a long, long time.

"Oh shit!" Garth said.

He got up, grabbed a coffee pot and stumbled to the man's table.

"God that kid is stoned. He has a nice little ass though."

"He does?"

"That's what I like to call jailbait," Rosy said.

"Have you ever licked a butt?" Boner asked.

"Done what?"

"You know, tossed a salad, rimmed a dude, eaten ass cake for dessert. They aren't as dirty as you think."

"I know that, I just . . . listen, we don't need to get to know each other in this way."

Rosy went back into the kitchen. Boner sat and looked at the Battleship board. He could have won. He had only one ship, but it was a small ship, a sneaky ship.

He felt a hand grip his shoulder. He turned. It was Jake. His eyes looked intense.

For a moment, Boner felt nervous and he didn't know why.

"Hey," Jake said.

Boner smiled. "Wanna play Battleship?"

"Sure."

Jake sat next to him. They took apart the last game and set up for a new round. Jake took his time. He seemed focused. Too focused. It was as if they were playing chess and not Battleship.

"I've been studying Battleship for a long time," Jake said.

"Me too," Boner said, though he had no idea what he meant by studying. How do you study Battleship? Boner had been playing the game since he was a kid. Did that count?

"You ready to start?" Boner asked.

Jake nodded.

"You go first," Boner said.

"J-6," Jake said.

Shit . . . he hit his tiny ship. He hit his tiny ship in the first move.

It was Boner's turn now.

He looked at the board. How did things get this intense? *Why am I so nervous? It's just a game*, he reminded himself.

"B-7."

"Miss," Jake said.

"Your turn," Boner said.

"J-7."

Hit. Boner's tiny ship was done.

The game was short. With the tiny ship annihilated in the first round, Boner didn't have much of chance. His confidence was raisin-sized.

They finished the game quickly. Boner leaned against the counter. Rosy noticed how pouty Boner looked and she brought him an ice cream cone. That cheered him up a bit.

"Any progress on the case?" Jake asked.

"Oh yeah. I met with that Moonbeam girl last night."

"You did? How did that go?"

"It was interesting."

"I think she might be the one behind all this."

"You do?"

"She's a very disturbed girl," Jake said. "We used to date."

"You did? You ever lick her butt?"

"We weren't terribly sexual in that way. We kissed, and it was very passionate. I had to carry chapstick around with me, in case my lips got chapped."

"Why did you break up?"

"I don't know. It just didn't work out. I figured it was a fairly peaceful break up. But then I started getting prank calls."

"From who?" Boner asked.

"From her."

"Oh, right. So she was mad at you."

Boner wanted to be a good listener. But he also wanted to focus on his ice cream cone. He didn't want it to melt. So he kept eye contact with Jake as he ran his tongue around the ice cream. It felt erotic. Too erotic. Boner felt uncomfortable and took the whole glob of ice cream in his mouth at once. That made things feel even more erotic. He felt like he was deep throating the ice cream. Plus it hurt his teeth. By the time he swallowed it, he got a brain freeze. He was in agony.

"Are you okay?" Jake asked.

"I'm fine. Go on . . . "

He wanted to cry out in pain. He wanted to stick his head in the vat of soup Rosy was cooking. Anything to make the pain stop.

Boner slammed his fist against the counter. His chubby cheeks shook. He couldn't take it. He cried out. It was a mighty cry. Rosy, Garth, and Jake looked over at him.

"You okay?" Jake asked again.

The pain finally started to subside.

"Brain freeze. I'm okay though. Man, that was intense."

"You ate that ice cream really fast."

"It hurt for a while, but now I feel awesome. Man, what a rush."

He looked at Jake and smiled. "Tell me more about this chick stalking you."

"Well, at first I would just hear heavy breathing," Jake went on. "Then she started getting intense. Once she called and said that she could see me."

"That's hilarious."

"It was terrifying."

"That too. Man, I would never have guessed that she would be the type to do that. She just seemed nerdy to me."

"Things aren't always as they seem. I think she's involved with the rapists somehow. I think she sent them after me."

"What makes you think that?"

"Last night, some guys were following me home. I heard them mention her name."

"Did they try and rape you?"

"No."

"Then how do you know they're rapists?"

"I could just tell."

"Were they fat and really nerdy?"

"No, they were big. Strong. Dressed like that guy from Limp Bizkit."

"I also met with The Doctor," Boner said. "He didn't know anything about the rapists."

"Yeah, I didn't think he would."

"Then why was he on the list?"

"I figured he would just make a good informant."

Boner nodded, pretending he knew what an informant was. He made a mental note to look it up on the internet later.

"You wanna play another round of Battleship?" Jake asked.

"No. That game was emotional for me."

"I'm sorry."

Jake's demeanor changed very suddenly. He looked oddly sweet and sympathetic.

"What are you doing today?"

"Just working on your case," Boner said.

"Take a break," Jake said. "You seem like you've been working hard. Come see a movie with me?"

"*Rocky vs. Rambo?*"

"Sure. I'll pay."

Boner reached his hand out. "You got a deal," he said.

16

They went to the small movie theater on Duvalle Street. It only showed two movies a night. One new, one old. That night it was playing *Rambo vs. Rocky* and *Nightmare on Elm Street II*. A real classic.

Boner and Jake were the only adults there. But Boner didn't mind. He thought teenagers were funny. They were fun to watch movies with.

Boner drank a massive tub of diet soda while watching the movie. It was delicious. But problematic. The movie was emotional and action packed. He didn't want to miss a second of it. But he had to pee. It became excruciating. When the movie ended, Boner ran to the bathroom. As he peed he cried out in triumph the same way Rocky did at the end of the film.

"Are you okay?" Jake asked him when they met outside of the theater.

"Better than ever," Boner said. "Peeing can be so much fun."

They walked out of the theater so excited Boner was practically skipping.

"That was such a profound film," Jake said.

"It had such cool fight scenes," Boner said. "And it was so sad. I loved how at the end they just held each other crying in the center of the ring. It was so emotional. That's how I felt as I was peeing."

"It *was* emotional. It's a great piece about man's duality."

Boner didn't know what he was talking about. Duality? He thought it was just about two dudes fighting. That was all.

17

Boner went back to the park where his minivan waited for him. He snuggled into his pillow-filled hot tub. Hanging out with that guy had exhausted him. He felt depleted. Usually he was able to watch a movie before falling asleep. That night he was just too tired. He turned on *The Karate Kid*. He fell asleep before Daniel even got to meet Mr. Miyagi. He had bad dreams. He dreamt he was one of the bullies. But the roles were reversed. Daniel was beating up on them. It was awful.

He woke up sweating.

It was early.

He finished watching the movie hoping it would give his mind some peace. Then he tried to go back to bed.

Old man Boli woke him up at around eight.

"You want a smoke?" he asked.

"Yeah, I do."

"Really?"

"Really."

They sat on the bumper of the minivan and smoked together. Neither of them talked much. It was a cool foggy morning. There was a slight drizzle. Not many people visited the park. Too wet. After the smoke, Boner was able to fall back to sleep without the sound of cars starting their engines and kids screaming.

18

Boner spent a few days trying to get back in Moonbeam's good graces. He spent hours upon hours sitting in the passenger seat with the keyboard pressed into his belly, staring at Moonbeam's Facebook page. He found funny YouTube videos about role playing and posted it on her wall. She responded to most of her posts. But she seemed distant. One day, while he was eating dry Lucky Charms, he got the guts to ask her to hang out. She said she couldn't. She said she was busy. He hated that. He covered himself with the tall pillows and lay on the bottom of the hot tub. He stayed there for a while feeling sorry for himself.

Hours passed. He got up. It was four in the afternoon. He felt sluggish and lazy. He felt lazy to a level that even he wasn't comfortable with.

Usually, when Boner needed to shower, he went to his grandma's and snuck into her shower. That day he drove down the mountain to a hidden section of the creek. He jumped into the water. It was cold and exhilarating. He sprayed his head with shampoo, mushed it into his hair until his head looked like it was covered in whip cream. He then dove down and swirled around in the murky depths and shook his head until it was rinsed clean.

It felt good. Showers usually made him feel dainty. But bathing in the creek made him feel strong somehow.

19

Usually Boner only drank at house parties or The Grimy Diner. But that day he went to the Dirty D to get a drink. The Dirty D was a man's bar. It was dark and looked brutally worked over by man ass and spilt beer. It was manly there, but boring. No one looked interested in chatting with Boner. So, after he drank his appletini he went to his minivan and called The Doctor. The Doctor said they were partying and that he should come over.

Boner drove to The Doctor's slowly, hoping not to get caught driving drunk. He had never driven drunk before. When he got to The Doctor's he felt like he had won a race. What a manly day it had been. First he bathed in the creek, then he got drunk in the daytime in a dive bar, and then he drove home drunk.

He walked into The Doctor's and found the house overrun by thuggy teenagers. They weren't breaking anything. Or stealing anything, but they didn't seem friendly either. They were all drinking out of large Coke bottles.

He tried to introduce himself. Only one thug acknowledged

him. He had the same body type as Boner but he dressed like he spent all day at the gym.

"What's with the suit?" the large thug asked.

"I like to look professional," Boner said.

"What's with the bald ass head?"

"I don't know."

They passed around a blunt. Everyone looked stoned. Too stoned.

Where the fuck are the girls? Boner thought. *Where the fuck's The Doctor?*

He stood with the teenager thugs. It wasn't hard to fit in. All he had to do was stand there and not talk.

At one point someone passed him a blunt. He took a hit and coughed for a while. This was a mistake. Boner was now catatonically stoned.

Clitty came out of the bedroom. She wore a large sweatshirt but no pants. She didn't say hi to Boner. Boner attempted to make eye contact a few times. He even waved. Still, no response.

She reached up to put her hair in a ponytail. Her sweatshirt lifted slightly, revealing her naked butt and vagina.

"You're not wearing underpants," Boner said.

She didn't respond. No one responded. The teen thugs all caught a peek at the naked stuff, but they didn't act fazed. They seemed too determined to act unfazed. Boner was fazed. He was so fazed. He couldn't take his eyes off the bottom of her sweatshirt, waiting for it to lift again and show him vagina and ass.

"You are so pantless right now," Boner said.

No one acknowledged him.

"What are you all looking at?" Clitty said to the thug-teens.

Nothing, Boner thought. *They should be looking at your vagina area. But they aren't. It makes no sense.*

Each time her sweatshirt lifted up it was an angry little present. Boner stored the memory of her ass in his mind.

The Doctor called out to her from the bedroom. Boner couldn't understand what he was saying.

"You can go fuck yourself!" Clitty yelled. "I'm not even trying to mess with that bullshit. You creepy motherfucker. I'm not putting Rhino's pussy blood on my face. Acting like it's war paint . . . You all are a bunch of freaks."

A couple thugs giggled.

Clitty growled and ran up to one of them, snatched the cigarettes out of his hand and ran outside.

One of the other girls came out. It was Tiny. She had red marks under her eyes and a squiggly line on her forehead. Boner had never seen period blood before but he was sure that's what it was. She was also very naked. She wore only her Uggs.

"Clitty come back!" Tiny yelled. "This is fun! It's not as gross as it seems!"

Rhino came out as well. She was in her underpants. Her ass looked like it was chewing on her undies. Even the thugs couldn't help but stare at that. She had a red handprint going across her face. She looked drunk. She kept laughing and burping. She let out a crazed war cry and ran outside.

More yelling came from the bedroom.

The Doctor came out. Half his face was covered in red.

"Boner," he said. "These girls are crazy. They keep yelling at me and hurting my feelings and shit. I gotta jet, dog. You coming?"

"Sure. I guess."

The Doctor looked at the teen thugs. He gave a few of them big hugs.

"You guys watch my shit. Don't let the girls break nothing."

"We got your back, bro," one said.

The Doctor went to the kitchen and washed the pussy blood off his face. He motioned for Boner to follow him. They ran out the back door and snuck around the house. The girls were in the front. They looked crazed. Boner and The Doctor waited for the girls to go back inside and then they ran to Boner's minivan and drove off.

"What about all your friends?" Boner asked.

"They're fine," The Doctor said. "They'll guard my shit. Or fuck it all up if they get too drunk. Whichever. I don't care."

The Doctor was impressed with the minivan.

"When did you get this swagged-out beast of a car?"

Boner explained his appearance on TV.

"That's sick as hell," The Doctor said.

The Doctor turned on the TV and flipped through the channels. He sat in the hot tub fondling his gold chains.

Boner went to the passenger seat and checked Facebook. No messages. But he did notice Moonbeam had posted about modeling at a figure drawing class. He showed the post to The Doctor.

"We have to go to that," he said. "I love nerd pussy. It's some crazy pussy. They eat nothing but Hot Pockets and shit and that does some shit to their shit. It either makes them slimed out or they tight in all the good ways, for real. And they're gushy in the smushy area. I mean, devil dog-level creaming up my dick, knowwhatimsayingggg?"

"I think I do," Boner said. "She is very pretty."

"Let's go to this shit."

20

The figure drawing class was held at the community college, but there were so many old people it looked more like an arts and crafts class at a nursing home.

Boner saw Garth, from The Grimy Diner, sitting behind an easel.

"Hey Boner!" he yelled.

Boner waved back, but he was visibly shocked and embarrassed to be called 'Boner' in the middle of a figure drawing class. He waved back and then quickly took a seat. He pulled out a marble notebook. It was the closest thing to a sketchbook he had in the minivan. The Doctor didn't bother with a sketchbook. He sat next to Boner and just stared at Moonbeam as hard as he could.

She was up on a small stage, sitting on a fold out chair.

"Looking good," The Doctor called out to her.

Boner smiled at the old ladies, hoping his friendliness would make up for his buddy's behavior. It didn't. The old ladies looked upset. Two of them left. The instructor, a short man with a gray beard, looked intimidated by The Doctor. He left them alone.

"You are looking fine!" The Doctor said.

Still, the tension was unbearable. Boner almost wished the instructor would kick them out.

Luckily there was only ten minutes left of class. When it was over, Moonbeam put a robe on.

Boner got nervous. The Doctor was so inappropriate. He expected to find police outside. He figured some old lady had reported The Doctor and him for coming to the figure drawing class drunk, stoned, and horny. Surely there was a law against what they were doing.

But after class everyone congregated outside and there were no cops. Just old ladies talking about art.

Garth found him and introduced him to an older man who turned out to be Garth's father.

"This is one of the guys that comes to the diner," Garth said.

His father shook Boner's sweaty hand. "You know Rosy. She's a good woman, isn't she? You know we used to go together in high school?"

"That's awesome," Boner said.

"It *was* awesome."

"Boner's a private eye," Garth said.

"Is that true?"

Boner nodded.

"Do you need any training for that?"

"Sorta. It's kinda top secret."

"Of course. Can I see what you drew?"

Boner passed him his notebook. Garth's father looked at the drawing. He looked pleasantly surprised.

"Why did you draw her with pointy ears?" he asked.

"I know she's really into D&D and she likes to pretend she's an elf."

"What are all these swirls?"

"It's her magic."

"That's really neat."

There was an awkward silence.

"Well, it was nice meeting you," Garth's father said.

"You too."

"Later, Boner dude," Garth said.

The father and son walked to their car and drove off.

They were so nice. Did they even notice I was drunk? Boner wondered.

He looked for The Doctor. He was still inside. He was talking to Moonbeam.

"Yo Boner, we're going to go back to your van to party. Sound good?"

Moonbeam looked at him and smiled. "Is that okay?" she asked.

Boner nodded as hard as he could. His smile was extra goofy and sweet.

Moonbeam giggled.

"Let's go!" Boner said.

Finally, he thought. *I have a chance to get to know this sexy nerd and find out what the hell's going on with Jake.*

21

He never got to interrogate Moonbeam. He got too drunk and blacked out. The next morning he woke up on a table. A chandelier dangled overhead. He got up and stumbled around. The sliding door leading to the backyard was open. Small white petals blew into the house from the recently blossomed crab apple tree.

The house was fancy. Really fancy. The walls were covered with family photos. He didn't recognize the people in the photos.

What happened?

The last thing he remembered was being in the minivan with Moonbeam and The Doctor. The Doctor and Moonbeam started cuddling. It was some pretty risqué cuddling. He thought it was a group activity so he joined in. He put his hand on her waist but she pushed it away. He tried again. She called him gross and told him to stop.

He drank and watched them cuddle. That was the last thing he remembered.

Boner stumbled into the living room. He felt like he was in a museum. Everything was so fancy. He didn't want to touch anything.

"Hello!" he called out.

"MOTHERFUCKER!" someone yelled.

Boner fell to his knees and put his hands in the air.

"I'm sorry!" he yelled. "I didn't mean to trespass. I give up! Please don't lock me in your basement and torture me!"

He looked up and saw his buddy, The Doctor, walking down the staircase. He wore a silk bathrobe.

"Where are we?" Boner asked, putting his hands down. He got off his knees and sat on the couch. It was a nice couch. It made his butt feel fancy.

The Doctor slid down the banister and then sat on the couch next to Boner.

"Don't know. I blacked out."

"Me too. Do you think that girl roofied us?"

The Doctor laughed. "I doubt that."

They walked to the kitchen and found some bread and peanut butter. They were both relieved there was normal peanut butter and not that healthy stuff. Rich people usually liked healthy stuff. They couldn't stomach any of that. They needed normal. It was white bread, too. They made sandwiches and feasted.

The Doctor showed Boner the shower. There were eight showerheads. Four on the walls. Two on the ceiling. Two on the floor.

"This fancy future shower is dope as hell," The Doctor said. "Let's shower before the rich folks come back."

"I don't know. I think we should just leave," Boner said.

"Not an option. I need to hit future shower right now. So do you. Let's do this."

"Together?"

"Don't be homophobic."

They stripped down and hopped in the shower. The water was the perfect temperature. They didn't have to adjust the nozzles. It was as if it could read their minds.

"You got a thick dick," The Doctor said. "Usually fat dudes got these tiny dingalings. Yours is looking fine though."

"Thanks. That means a lot."

"Damn this shower is nice as fuck."

Boner grabbed a bar of soap. It looked like rock candy. It smelled like it too. He rubbed it on his thick dick. It felt cool.

"Did we all have sex last night?" Boner asked.

"What kind of shit . . . no, man. I got three girlfriends. That means I would have cheated three times. That means I would have four chicks ready to break my heart. Naw. I just gave her some cuddle action is all."

"You're in love with all your girlfriends?"

"No, but that doesn't mean they can't break my heart. I'm a sensitive motherfucker."

"Which one do you like the most?"

"Rhino. When she takes her clothes off . . . somehow she looks more naked than other girls do."

Boner smiled. "That's cool."

The Doctor laughed. It was a soft, affectionate laugh.

Boner looked at him. His back was covered in muscles and tattoos and acne scars. His ass was cloud colored and covered in peach fuzz.

"You can touch it if you want," the Doctor said, noticing.

"Really?"

"Go for it. I got the best ass in the world. The thing defies gender rules."

Boner rubbed it. It was soft. It made him wish girls had more hair on their butts.

After they showered they went back downstairs and had a couple more sandwiches. The food helped at first, but quickly started to make them feel worse.

The driveway leading out of the mansion went on for what seemed like eternity. The hedges were well trimmed. There were iron statues of children playing. It felt eerie. As they passed by Boner imagined they were once real children who had been turned to iron by a witch.

Eventually they got to the gate. They pressed a red button and it opened. It was another mile down a dirt road before they reached Route 30.

"Shit, how'd we get twenty miles from town?" he said.

"Don't know. I didn't even know there were any houses out here. That fancy place is really hidden. Maybe it belongs to a superhero or something?"

The Doctor's phone was dead.

"Don't you have a cell phone?" he asked Boner.

"No. I have a car phone. Or it's more like a minivan phone."

"That's fucking dumb. I hate that stupid thing."

They began down the road. Most of it was downhill.

"Are you sure you don't know how we got here?" The Doctor

asked.

"I'm sure."

They kept walking. The road twisted and seemed endless. Eventually they came out of the woods and found themselves overlooking farmland.

The Doctor put out his thumb to passing cars, but nobody picked them up.

After a few hours they came to a gas station. Boner was famished. He bought three packs of Devil Dogs and two large bottles of red Gatorade.

The Doctor managed to convince the grouchy old man behind the register to let him use the phone for ten bucks. He called his buddy Darrell.

They sat in the parking lot and ate the Devil Dogs and waited. It took Darrell an hour to get there.

Nobody talked on the ride back. Everyone was too annoyed.

They got back to The Doctor's at five and found the minivan parked in the yard. The back door was open. Boner looked inside. His hot tub was filled with water. Pillows floated in the cold water like seaweed. He turned a lever on the side of the tub. This made the water drain out from a spout that was between the back tires, making it look like the minivan was peeing. He then took the soaked pillows out and threw them in the woods. He tried to turn his TV on but it was broken. The hot tub had overflowed and most of the gadgets in the back didn't work.

There was a note from Moonbeam thanking them for the good time and apologizing for puking in the hot tub. *Weird*, Boner thought, *I hadn't even noticed.*

22

Too much partying. Way too much partying. Boner couldn't take much more. He had to take a mini vacation at his grandma's.

Boner's mother was out of the picture. Had been for a long time. He had been raised by his grandma. Her name was Luba. She was ancient. There were rumors she was over a hundred years old, but she defied age. She looked fifty, at most. The only way you could tell she was at least that old was by her exes. Most of them were dead. The survivors didn't age as well—most were in nursing homes, grabbing the asses of nurses. Luba exercised constantly. She ate healthy. There were people around town who thought she was a vampire and was going to live forever.

She had a nice home right on the creek. It looked like an ordinary farmhouse. But the inside was fancy. Marble counter tops. Original artwork. Oil paintings of naked body builders.

As soon as Boner got there he sat on the couch and turned on her new flat-screen TV.

"You want to go for a run with me?" she asked.

Her leg was up in the couch. She was stretching.

Boner couldn't help but notice how nice his grandma's legs were. He wished she wore baggier clothes. He wished she wore sweatpants and khakis like a normal old lady. He was uncomfortable with her short shorts. The bottom of her ass hung out at times and it made Boner feel confused.

"Why is this TV so complicated?" he asked.

"You'll figure it out."

Boner gave up and went to the pantry. It was filled with snacks. Oatmeal cookies. Oreos, Double Stuffed. Donuts. Ding Dongs. Twinkies. Twizzlers. Every kind of Girl Scout cookie imaginable. Fluff. Jelly donuts. And a jar of peanut butter the size of an elephant's heart.

He grabbed the Oreos and poured a massive bowl of milk. He sat and ate and watched TV. He took two Oreos at a time, dunked them in the bowl of milk, and watched the bubbles rise. When the bubbles stopped coming, it meant the Oreos had become nice and soft. He then carefully lifted the softened Oreos out of the bowl and ate them. If he wasn't careful, the cookie would fall apart and become chocolate seaweed in the bowl. He did this until he was out of cookies. He fell asleep.

When he woke up it was night. He was in bed. Had his grandma carried him in? *Shit. That's intense. How did she get so strong?*

He was still tired. He thought about eating more cookies but fell asleep again.

<h1 style="text-align:center">23</h1>

Grandma made intense spaghetti. It was a massive pile of meat and noodles. She used steak, chicken, shrimp, clams, squid, and all sorts of veggies. She called it Shit Stack Meat Mountain. Boner ate three big servings of the slop.

"Are you trying to make me fat?" he asked.

"Listen to me, you chunky thing, don't you ever feel insecure about your weight. Some women like that big stuff. They like to get crushed. They like to jiggle the flub. They like a guy with a big appetite. They think it's romantic. Now slurp up those juicy noodles until your belly hurts."

"Gross."

"Besides, one day your metabolism is going to kick in. And you'll be like me."

"I really doubt it, Grandma. I'm thirty years old. That's old. My metabolism doesn't even work anymore."

"You're my grandson and I have the best metabolism on the

planet. Look at me. I eat like a pig but don't have an inch of body fat on my body."

"You don't eat like a pig. And even if you did, you exercise all the time. You're practically exercising right now."

His Grandma was tapping her foot at a rapid pace. It was obvious she was fighting the urge to run or do squats. If she could eat and exercise at the same time, she would. But she knew it wasn't polite. When she was alone though, things got wild. She was a fiend. She loved to exercise. When she wasn't exercising, she was cleaning.

"I think you make a good fatty and that you shouldn't be so critical of yourself."

"I'm not," Boner said. "I just think I could have more girlfriends if I was more model-ish."

"Probably true. But girlfriends are a pain in the ass. Boyfriends are even worse."

Boner finished his meal and went to the couch, lay down and turned on a movie. His grandmother got on the couch with him. She laid her head against his chest. She listened to his heavy breath. When Boner was young she told him cuddling was the best exercise. If only this was true.

24

Boner went to his minivan and checked his messages. The monitor on the center console told him he had three missed calls. One from The Doctor, one from Clitty, and one from Jake. He didn't want to party. He was partied out for the time being, so he didn't call the Doctor or Clitty. He didn't want to call Jake either. But it was his job. He had to be professional.

He called Jake up and invited him over.

Jake had a movie with him. *Rocky vs. The Terminator.*

Grandma Luba came home from her night run. She looked especially sweaty and toned. Boner was worried Jake would creep her out. But Jake was surprisingly polite and charming.

"You have incredible deltoids," Jake told her.

"Why thank you. I have been really working on toning them recently. You work out?"

"Kung Fu."

"Neat."

She asked him what he did for work. Boner had never thought of this. How did this kid make money? He looked like a gym teacher but Boner doubted that's what he actually did.

"I'm a weapons dealer," he said.

"A what?"

"I sell fantasy weapons. Swords. Spears. Stuff like that. I sell it to people who are into role-playing. Some of the weapons are made out of foam."

Boner remembered seeing a giant sword hanging from Moonbeam's wall. Maybe she bought it from him. Maybe it was a present.

"That is so neat," Grandma Luba said.

"It's more lucrative than you would imagine," Jake said.

Before she went to her room, she winked at Boner and gave him a thumbs up, signaling that she approved of his friend.

Jake and he watched another Rocky movie and then spent the rest of the night talking about the case. Nothing new. Jake went over the same info. He went through it over and over again. It became dizzying. Men followed him home. For some reason they never actually attacked. Jake was sure they wanted to rape him. Moonbeam was involved somehow.

Boner tried to change the subject. He brought up exercise. He said he wanted to lose weight. He said it would make him a more effective private investigator. This wasn't fully true. Boner did want to look better. He knew he needed to exercise.

"I'm going to teach you Kung Fu," Jake said.

"Kung Fu, that's awesome."

They went to work the next day. Grandma Luba had a large exercise room in the basement. She was more than willing to let them use it.

They trained all day. Boner was surprised by how much fun it was. It was the least boring thing he had ever done.

At one point they went to the creek to practice. Jake had Boner stand in the current and practice weird Kung Fu moves.

"This will help you with balance," he said.

When they finished training, Jake had him watch *Rocky 19*, the one where Rocky becomes a ninja. He got so hyped he started jumping around, shadow boxing things.

Grandma saw him jump kicking the couch. She started cheering.

"Go! Get that couch!" she yelled.

She was so proud of him.

25

That week Grandma Luba had her boyfriend, Gerald, come over. He was younger. He looked like a buff version of Bill Cosby. He was charming and told lots of funny jokes over dinner. Boner thought he was hilarious. Jake didn't like him. He didn't laugh at his jokes.

Gerald heard they had been practicing Kung Fu. He said he had been practicing Kung Fu for twelve years.

He went to the studio and tried to practice with them, but he didn't recognize any of the moves.

"We've been practicing a very obscure style," Jake said.

"Oh, hey, that's cool. Do you want me to show you some moves I know?" Gerald asked.

Boner liked that idea. Jake said he wasn't interested. He went upstairs.

Boner practiced with Gerald. His style was so different. And hard. Super hard. Within ten minutes Boner felt like he was about to pass out.

"Your style is too hard," he said, hyperventilating.

"It's the most basic form of Kung Fu."

He gave Boner a friendly pat on the back and then went up-stairs. Boner lay on the mat, breathing heavy and sweating. He hurt. He hurt all over.

26

At Grandma Luba's Boner slept in a bunk bed. Jake slept on the top bunk, with Boner on the bottom. It was dark. There were green glow-in-the-dark stars and planets on the wall.

Sex sounds came from Grandma's room. Gerald was really hauling away.

"Gerald's style of Kung Fu is really hard," Boner said.

"I'm sure he's just not a very good teacher," Jake said.

"What style of Kung Fu have we been learning?"

"It's a new style," Jake said.

"What's it called? I want to look it up on the internet."

"You won't find it on the internet. It's that new."

"Just tell me what it's called."

"It's called Jake style," Jake explained.

"What's that?" Boner asked.

"It's a style I invented."

"But you know normal Kung Fu."

"A little."

Boner wanted to cry. For the past three days he had been con-

90

vinced he was becoming a Kung Fu master.

Jake tried to defend his style. He explained all the moves. None of it made any sense to Boner. Jake then tried to talk about the case. But Boner was too sad. He ignored him and pretended to sleep.

In the morning Boner decided to get firm with Jake.

"Listen," Boner said. "I'm not feeling too well. I think I'm sick. I think you should go home."

"Okay, I'll call you soon. About the case."

"Sure."

"Do you want to practice more Kung Fu soon?"

"I don't know."

"You should. You're getting really good."

"Maybe."

Boner watched Jake drive off in his Volkswagen, then made himself a massive bowl of cereal. His grandma came out and joined him.

"I like that Jake kid," she said.

"He's creepy," Boner said.

"Is he? I couldn't tell."

"You never can."

"What's that supposed to mean? You usually like the men I bring over. I never bring over anyone that makes you uncomforta-ble and you know that."

Boner started crying. His grandmother didn't bother asking him what was wrong. She patted him on the back and let him go nuts for a little while.

27

Boner spent the next three days eating Oreos and thinking about the case. He knew Jake's side of the story. He had heard it over and over again. It just didn't make sense to him. Moonbeam was weird, but she wasn't malicious. Who were these thugs she was sending after him? Were they weird rape-nerds?

He decided to friend more of them on Facebook. None of them seemed sketchy, at least not in a dangerous way. They were all nerds, each one of them. They may have eaten too many Hot Pockets and stink like a pile of toe jams but they weren't dangerous. Even if they did want to rape Jake, Boner doubted they could overpower him. Jake was strong. His Kung Fu was make-believe, sure, but he had muscles. Lots of them. Moonbeam and her nerds were just not a very scary group.

He decided to get in contact with her anyway. Usually Boner tried to be smooth and discreet on Facebook. But he didn't have any patience for that.

"You ever date Jake Reed?" he messaged her.

She responded later that night.

Moonbeam: *Yes, I did. Why?*

Boner: *Cause he say's you've been stalking him.*

Moonbeam: *What? No. I have no idea what the eff he is talking about. I dated him for a week. He was super creepy. A complete clinger. And we never even did it. Not really. He couldn't stay hard. He used to get so whiny about it. He once said that it was my fault. He said my pussy was possessed by a demon and that I needed to see an exorcist. So I broke up with him. Who says that kind of thing to a girl? He's so sketch. Once I went into his house and he was polishing a knife. I kept trying to get his attention. He just stared at the knife. He didn't acknowledge me. A half hour went by. Finally he looked up. He acted all surprised to see me even though he had invited me over and I had been sitting there for like a half hour.*

Boner: *Do you have any brother or sister that might be mad at him for saying you have demon pussy?*

Moonbeam: *I'm an only child. And even if I did have siblings, I wouldn't have told them that. It's embarrassing. You're the only person I have told. You better not tell anyone by the way.*

Boner: *I won't. I'm really good at keeping secrets.*

Moonbeam: *I gotta go. I'm playing Warcraft.*

Boner: *Go get em tiger.*

Moonbeam put up an emoticon of a confused smiley face.

Go get him tiger? What was I thinking? Boner thought.

He shrugged off his embarrassment easily though. He had finally been able to get some real information. He had been assertive. He felt professional. He was finally starting to get the knack of this whole detective thing. There was nothing conclusive, or that made any sense really, but he felt like a chunky Dick Tracy, or Sherlock Holmes. He was like that Lady from *Murder, She Wrote*. Or maybe Magnum PI.

28

Boner cleaned up his minivan and drove over to The Doctor's. The girls and he were sitting around watching movies. Boner told them about Moonbeam's demon pussy. They all fell over laughing. It was the funniest thing any of them had heard in a long time.

"Jake wanted her to see an exorcist."

There was another eruption of laughter.

"Who cares if that pussy possessed?" Clitty said. "I wish my pussy was possessed by a demon. That shit would be cool."

"That thing is possessed," The Doctor said. "And I exorcise it nightly."

"Right," Rhino Booty said. "That's if exorcism involved nothing but smoking weed and watching Rocky movies all night while eating Lucky Charms out of the box."

"I love Lucky Charms," The Doctor said. "That shit is swag as hell. That shit is dope. I want to swim in a bowl of that marshamallowy goodness."

"Dude," Tiny said. "I once saw this movie about an exorcist. I can't remember what it's called though."

"*The Exorcist?*" Boner said.

"Yeah, that's it. That movie scared me."

"I watched it with my mom when I was, like, six," Clitty said.

"You watched that with your mom?"

"She freakin' loved horror movies. We watched all of them. My favorite was *Alien*."

Rhino shook her head. "That's so weird. I was watching *ET* back then."

"I saw *ET*. But I didn't like it. It freaked me out. I didn't like how the boy and the alien got sick at the same time. It was creepy."

The Doctor lit a blunt, took a nice, long, dramatic pull, and exhaled.

"You could watch *Alien* when you were young but you couldn't handle *ET*? That is some psychologically loaded shit."

"I'm a psychologically loaded girl."

Clitty passed the blunt to Boner, who was sitting on the floor. He took a hit and coughed. Tiny walked up to him and crawled up on his shoulders. Boner passed her the blunt. She took a hit.

Boner thought about Moonbeam and her vagina. What if it really was possessed by a demon? The case was getting intense. He was in way over his head. Now he was an exorcist too. Should he charge extra for that?

Rain drummed on the windows. The Doctor turned off the TV. They listened to the rain intensify and then gradually loosen its hold on them.

29

Rosy was singing and dancing around The Grimy. The teenage boys thought she was being hilarious. Boner was their only customer and she didn't care. Usually she hated when Boner was the only customer. Usually, when business was slow, she got anxious and irritable and asked the wait staff to go home. Not that day. Boner was her only customer all day and she didn't care. She didn't even really acknowledge that he was a customer at all.

"I want meatloaf! Please! I'm so hungry!" he pleaded with her.

She ran up and tickled him. "You are a big loaf of meat," she said.

He laughed and begged her to stop.

She continued dancing. The boys continued watching.

Boner watched her as well. After a half hour the hunger got to him though, and he started moaning and whining.

"We should feed him," Garth said.

"You're probably right," Rosy said.

A sense of relief filled Boner. His eyes widened. He waited for Rosy to go to the kitchen. He wanted to hear cooking sounds. Instead, she walked over to the cd player and put on old show tunes, continuing to sing and dance.

"Well, aren't you going to cook him his meatloaf?" Garth asked.

"I don't feel like it," she said. "You do it."

Garth had never cooked meatloaf before. But he went to the kitchen and started working on it. The other sexy waiters and bus boys watched. They had seen Rosy make her meat loaf hundreds of times. They each remembered a little about the process. So they joined him and helped out.

There was a lot of screaming and laughing and banging of pots and pans and it seemed like they were conducting a science experiment rather than cooking a simple meat loaf.

Once they were done, they brought the whole loaf to Boner. It was an ugly, mangled little thing. Boner dug his fork into it. He let the loaf cool before he ate it.

"This tastes awesome," he said with the food still in his mouth, hidden behind his chubby smile.

Rosy came up to the boys and wrapped her flabby arms around her waiters all at once, giving them a massive bear hug. "When You Walk Through the Storm" was playing. She was singing the lyrics. Her voice was sad. She let the boys go. She grabbed a broom, cleaning and singing. The boys helped.

30

Boner met Jake at Super Scoops. Back in the day people used to park and order on little intercoms, and have pretty waitresses on roller skates bring ice cream to their car. Now there were cracks covering the parking lot and grass and weeds grew out of the cracks, making roller skating treacherous. The intercoms were all broken and ancient. But the ice cream stand stayed open. They still had good ice cream.

Boner and Jake went up to the window. An attractive teenage girl brought them their orders. They tipped her and then went to a picnic table under the sign—an old and faded cartoon of a soft serve ice cream wearing a cape. *Who drew that thing?* Boner wondered.

The creek was nearby. They could hear the water moving.

Jake started talking about the case. He rambled on about who the men still stalking him were, how they were still trying to rape him. He was sure Moonbeam was behind it.

"Moonbeam's a nice girl," Boner said. "I doubt she would sic rapists on you."

"She's not as nice as you think!" he shouted.

"Fine, but I've spoken to her about everything and she doesn't seem to have any idea what you are talking about."

"She called me last night," he said. "She called me and she told me she could see me. I looked out my window and she was just standing there."

"Really? I don't know. That sounds odd. I don't think she even has a cell phone."

"Yes, she does. Trust me."

"No. I'm pretty sure she doesn't."

A fat man on a Harley pulled up. He walked up to one of the old intercoms. He played with it for a moment before realizing it was broken. He looked sad. The man then walked up to the window and ordered a massive soft serve covered in rainbow sprinkles. He sat and ate slowly. Jake kept talking. Boner ignored him. He raised his cone. The biker raised his. It was a silent toast.

31

The Doctor had bought fifty cans of whip cream. At first Boner thought they were for cake or hot chocolate. Or maybe they were going to make a whip cream mountain. His grandma made great whip cream mountains.

"We're doing whip-its," The Doctor said.

"What's that?"

"You just spray the nitrous out and you suck it all in."

Boner tried it out. It made him dizzy. It made him happy. It made him giggle.

We didn't make a whip cream mountain. We made a giggle mountain, Boner thought.

32

Boner's grandma called him every day. Sometimes she called up to five times a day and always left messages. They were never guilt trippy or pushy. Usually she just joked with him. She told him great dirty jokes. He listened to the jokes and laughed, but refused to call her. When he thought about her and her massive pile of spaghetti and all those Oreos and milk, he felt neutered. He needed to stay away from that old lady for a while. He needed to be on his own.

One day she gave Rosy a cake to give to Boner.

"She's always trying to make me fat," Boner said. "She makes me feel like Hansel and Gretel."

"She's better to you than she was to your mother."

"I know."

They ate the cake. The whole cake. When they were done they thought about calling his grandmother and asking for another one, but they decided against it.

33

Boner parked his minivan in town. He watched people walk by. They looked at his minivan like it was a porn shop, the naked warrior women intriguing them. They wanted to know what was inside. At the same time, they wanted to get far away. They knew whatever was in there was most likely lame and sweaty and stank.

Conca Pizza's neon sign shone brightly. The fog gave it a futuristic feel.

A beeping sound came from Boner's car computer. Moonbeam had messaged him on Facebook. He leaned over and read it. She invited him to go see a Harry Potter movie playing in town.

I will be there is a sec, he wrote.

He drove to her house and let himself in. Someone was in the kitchen. The smell of spaghetti filled the house. Boner got self-conscious and ran up to her room. He knocked on the door eagerly. She answered wearing a short red dress that showed off her pale legs.

"Where's The Doctor?" she asked.

"I don't know."

He smiled. He was happy to see her even though she was acting pretty hostile.

"Shit, I thought you were going to bring The Doctor. Well, did you at least bring any weed?"

"You smoke?"

"No, I was just really excited about trying it."

Boner had some weed. He walked down to his van. The holographic skulls on his minivan stared at him. He dug around the back seat. He found an old bag with some shake in it. He found his old pipe. It was a one-hitter disguised to look like a cigarette. He went back up to her apartment. They sat on her bed facing each other. He felt like he was smoking a peace pipe with the Chief of the Nerds. They each took a couple of hits and then she got very quiet. Boner put the weed away. He tried to engage conversation. She just stared at the wall.

"I don't think I can go to the movie," she said.

"Come on, it'll be fun. It's going to have so much magic."

"No, I'm too messed up."

"It'll make you feel better. That's how weed works. You got to do stuff. You got to go out and feel awkward. It's so fun."

"I don't want to! Leave me alone!"

She covered herself in blankets.

"Get out of my fucking house!"

He apologized for getting her too stoned. She didn't respond.

34

Boner met with The Doctor the next day. The girls were gone. Not knowing what to do without the girls, the two dusted off The Doctor's old Sony Playstation and started playing *Final Fantasy Seven*.

"I got a job," The Doctor told him while playing.

Boner was shocked.

"A real job? Like a really real job?"

"Yeah, the girls gave me a talk. They think it's lame that I still borrow money from my pop all the time."

"You borrow money from your dad?"

"Hell yeah, how else do you think I can afford all this shit?"

"I figured you sold drugs or robbed stuff."

The Doctor laughed. "Naw. I don't do that shit."

"So you have a really, really real job now."

"I'm going to work at the Exxon. Don't worry though. That shit won't change me."

"I hope not."

Clitty came home and joined in playing video games. The action made her horny. Soon The Doctor and her snuck off to the bedroom.

Boner stayed. He continued playing the game. Night came. The sex sounds had been replaced by snoring. Boner felt awkward just hanging out there but he stayed. He was too deep in the game. He had to finish.

35

Rhino Booty and Tiny came home. They sat and watched Boner play. They weren't as entertained as Clitty had been and kept commenting on how bored they were.

The Doctor's cell phone rang. He had left it on the couch. They ignored it. It started ringing over and over again, 'Unknown Number' displayed on the screen.

"Should we answer it?" Boner asked.

Rhino shrugged. "Fuck it," she said.

She answered the phone, and then handed it to Boner.

"It's for you . . ."

She looked confused and concerned.

Boner took the phone and held it up to his ear.

It was Gerald.

"How did you get this number?" Boner asked.

"I looked all around town asking if anyone knew where you were. I found Jake. He told me you might be with some guy called The Doctor. He gave me the number."

"Why were you looking for me?"

The girl watched as Boner's eyes widened. He hung up the phone and then burst into tears. Rhino Booty sat next to him on the floor. She put his head on her lap. Tiny ran up to The Doctor's room and got him.

"What the fuck's going on? I was trying to get my beauty sleep!" he yelled.

He saw Boner sobbing.

"What happened, dude?"

Boner tried to pull himself together. But he fell apart again.

"Grandma Luba died!"

He cried and screamed and thrashed his limbs around. He looked like a giant baby. It scared Tiny and Clitty a little.

"Shit . . . " The Doctor said.

It went on like this for a while. The Doctor and the women watched, not knowing how to calm him. Boner seemed to have an infinite supply of tears and screaming in him.

Then, very suddenly, it stopped. He stood up and slowly walked to the couch. He sat on the leather couch, staring off. The Doctor and the girls kept asking if he was okay. He kept nodding and saying he was fine.

"What happened?" Rhino asked.

"She was visiting her sister in Maine. She went surfing and had a heart attack. She drowned."

Clitty smiled. "You're grandma surfed? That's awesome."

Boner nodded.

"I was so close to the end of the video game," he said. "I could have beaten it. Now this happened. I'll never play this game ever again!"

He started crying again. He looked like a little kid that had gotten lost in the supermarket.

36

There were a lot of men at the funeral. Boner's grandma didn't know many women. Except for Rosy. She was there. They all gathered around the grave and listened to the young, awkward preacher say kind words. He had known her briefly and his impression of her was not far off. But he was a born rambler. He went on and on with little charisma.

It started to rain. At first Boner liked that. But then it began to pour. People started to run to their cars. Boner stayed. He figured the weather would subside. All he had to do was wait it out. Soon the sun would come out. That's what the weather was like. It was erratic.

But the rain kept coming.

Soon he was the only one left. The preacher stayed. He continued to preach.

37

Boner met up with Jake at The Grimy. He told him he couldn't continue with the case. He was surprised by how well he took it.

"I understand," Jake said.

"Do you want your money back?"

"No, you did all you could."

They drank soda and talked about movies. The mood was light, casual. Boner enjoyed talking about the movies instead of death. He enjoyed overanalyzing Rocky movies. He enjoyed thinking intensely about things that didn't require much thought.

They ate and played a game of Battleship. Jake won, but Boner put up a good fight.

They were in the middle of the second game when Jake's mood suddenly shifted. His eyes widened. He looked anxious.

"Did you hear what those dudes just said?"

"No, what?"

"They said they want to rape me."

Boner looked around. There was nobody there. Rosy was in the kitchen. So was Garth. It was just Jake and him. They were the only customers. There were no men. No rapists. The boy was hearing voices. They were imaginary. *Had they always been imaginary?* Boner wondered. *Have I been chasing make believe rapists?*

His heart sank.

"Why can't I ever feel safe?" Jake said.

"I don't know," Boner told him.

38

Boner was too sad to keep living in his minivan. Gerald offered to put him up for a while. So did Rosy. But he knew they only wanted him to live with them temporarily. Eventually they would want him to get a job and his own place. Boner wasn't into that so he decided to go live with his other grandma, Francine, in Easthampton, New York.

He had a going away party at The Grimy Diner. They made him a cake. But he really just wanted more meatloaf. He felt bratty and sad and lonely.

Everything in that town looked rundown. He just wanted to leave. He wanted to live somewhere new. Somewhere fancy, and clean.

PART

TWO

<h1 style="text-align:center">39</h1>

Boner was hanging out in his buddy's back yard, working out. That's where he spent most of his time. Since moving in with his other grandma he had made a bunch of friends, all weightlifters. They rented out a McMansion. It was nice, but there were nine of them, so they could afford the rent. The back yard was filled with equipment.

Boner liked weightlifting. It made him feel strong and durable. It helped him sleep more soundly. It also enabled him to eat more. He had been working out for two months and he hadn't lost a pound. And he didn't care. He just wanted to work out and eat.

He had managed to lift 220 pounds. He was on his last rep.

"Come on!" Roy said. "PUSH! YOU CAN DO IT!"

Roy was so muscular. He looked like a giant meat boulder.

"DO IT!"

Boner's arms trembled. He screamed as he gave it one last push. He got all the way up. Roy took the bar and put it back on the hook.

"Nice job!" he said. "I barely had to help you."

Boner knew this wasn't true. Roy had helped considerably. Boner appreciated the gesture regardless.

His phone rang. It was Grandma Francine. She wanted him home for dinner.

"What are we having?" Boner asked.

"Baked ziti!"

"I love baked ziti!" Roy said.

"Can Roy come?"

Boner shook his head.

"Sorry man, she doesn't have enough."

"I understand."

There was more than enough ziti. Grandma Francine had baked two pans' worth.

"Why couldn't Roy come over? There's so much ziti."

"Those bodybuilders scare me."

"I'm a bodybuilder."

"I know you are, sweety. But you're . . . different."

She shoveled the cheesy noodles into her mouth. She was a big woman and she knew how to eat fast.

"Eat plenty of ziti. It's good for your handsomeness."

"What?"

"Ziti makes you more handsome. Everyone knows that."

Boner giggled. "I don't know about that."

After they finished eating, Boner got up to go to his minivan to watch a movie.

"You shouldn't go out there," Francine said. "It's dangerous."

"It's dangerous in your driveway?"

"I'm just saying it would be better if you stayed in here."

He looked at the puppy figurines all over the house. Grandma had hundreds of them. At night they looked like demons.

"Well, I got this movie I want to watch."

"You should watch it in here."

He gave in. He brought *Robocop vs. Leatherface* in from the van. Grandma Francine got so scared she hid under her blanket. Boner felt guilty about that.

Eventually she fell asleep on the couch. Boner tucked her in properly then went to his minivan.

40

It was Friday. Boner and Roy were bored. Boner decided to call his cousin Max and see what he was doing. Boner had called his cousin every day, but he had not picked up the phone. Boner was convinced his cousin's phone was broken. But that day he picked up. He actually answered. *He must have gotten his phone fixed,* Boner thought. He was excited. His cousin Max was so cool, he was like Zack from *Saved By The Bell* only with a bigger dick. At least that's what Max always told him. Boner had told Roy so many stories about his cousin. Like the time he made out with a girl for literally over four hours. Boner was there. He timed it. And then there was the time he was able to jerk off six times in one day. Boner was only able to do it four times before his dick started hurting. Max's dick was more durable.

"Who is this?" Max asked.

"It's your big cuz, Boner."

At first Max sounded confused. There was a loud noise in the background.

"Are you okay?" Boner asked.

"I'm sick dude. I'll call you soon."

Boner hung up.

"Well, the good news is his phone is working. The bad news is he's sick."

"That sucks," Roy said. "I hate getting sick."

Roy cracked his knuckles. "Whoever got him sick should get his ass kicked."

"We should make him soup," Boner said.

41

There were at least thirty cars in front of Max's place. Boner and Roy could hear music and laughter.

"What's going on?" Roy asked.

"I don't know," Boner said.

They got out and carried the soup up to the door. There was a group of kids hanging out in front.

"What's that?" they asked.

"Beef stew," Roy said.

"Is that code for something?" the kid asked.

Boner and Roy pushed past into the house and found Max sitting at the edge of the pool. He looked up and saw them holding the vat of soup.

"This is so uncool!" Roy yelled.

He put the soup down.

"I thought we were friends."

Max tried to apologize. But they rushed off to the minivan and drove away.

42

Boner spent the next couple weeks hiding out with his grandma watching *General Hospital.* He stopped working out. His muscles started to go away. He weakened. He had trouble sleeping at night.

He wanted to go home but he was broke. Grandma Francine wouldn't lend him a cent. She would buy him all the food he wanted. But when it came to money she was very stingy.

Eventually he sold his minivan. He got ten grand for it. He bought a used Honda and packed to go home.

"Visit again sometime," Grandma said.

Visit? Boner thought he had been living there for the past three months.

She hugged him in a way that felt extremely cordial. Then she went back to her couch.

43

To avoid traffic and the bridge maze that joins Long Island with the rest of the world, Boner took the Port Jeff ferry over to Bridgeport. It was a small, dismal city, but soon he found himself upstate, following his GPS into the Adirondacks.

Fall was in full effect. The leaves hung on the trees like prayer flags.

He took the long way home, taking twisting back roads, passing towns that looked like they had been worn out since they were born.

He got home to Burtonsville that night. He drove, first thing, to The Doctor's house. The Doctor was in his jammies. Still, he had Boner come in for a beer.

Boner noticed The Doctor wasn't wearing any gold.

"I sold that shit," he said.

The girls were also gone. The Doctor said they had broken up. Tiny moved to New York City. Rhino Booty went home to Ver-

124

mont. She was working on a farm and living with an old guy with a massive beard.

"At first I didn't think that old dude could handle that booty, but she wrote me and told me that he rocks it out at least three times a week and is very durable."

Clitty was apparently working as a prostitute and living in the Norblad Hotel.

"It's dark," he said. "Bitch lost her shit. I told her I could hook her up with a job at Exxon. She worked for me for like a week and then quit. And when she quit the job it was like she quit me too. Chicks are weird."

So much had changed. He told Boner he didn't like being called The Doctor anymore. He was just Tyler. He had been working and saving for a new place. He was feeling good.

Tyler had to work early the next morning so he had to cut the night short.

Boner drove up to Mash Potato Park and slept in his Honda for the night.

44

The Grimy Diner was closed. The restaurant was gutted. There was nothing but a big open room and a sign that said 'Sheila's Beauty Salon, coming soon.'

Why didn't anyone tell him?

He sat on the trunk of his Honda and felt a level of despair he hadn't felt since Grandma Luba's funeral.

Clitty found Boner sitting on the Honda. She looked fancy. He noticed she wore one of The Doctor's chains.

"You're back," she said. "How was your trip to The Hamptons?"

"Trip? It wasn't a trip. I lived there."

"Cool. Chill. Don't get your panties all bunched up your asshole. How was it?"

"It was cool. I got buff."

He flexed his arm. She felt his muscles.

"Nice work."

A girl walked by while they were talking. She said something nasty about Clitty. Clitty started cursing at her and saying all sorts of vile things. This cheered Boner up a bit.

The girl finally gave up and said she was calling the cops. Boner and Clitty took off and hid in her hotel room at the Norblad.

Her room was depressing. There was nothing on the walls. The only decoration was a pile of clothing in the corner. But the room had a TV.

She told him that *Roseanne* was back on the air.

"The show's awkward as fuck but I can't help but to watch it. I grew up watching that shit."

"Jacky still in it?" Boner asked.

"Yeah."

"She reminds me of my mom."

"Damn, that's kinda annoying. But kinda awesome too."

"Sorta. She was a bit more drunk than Jacky though."

"That's kinda awesome."

"You're really a whore now?"

"What? Don't call me that shit, ya fat fuck."

"I was just thinking I haven't gotten it on in a bit."

She looked offended at first, but then smiled.

"Can I just pay you to let me eat your butt a bit?"

"No."

"Why not?"

"'Cause if you eat my butt I'll get all horny. If I get all horny, I'll need to fuck."

"That makes sense."

Clitty lay on her tummy, her panties dangling from her left foot. Boner stuck his face in her butt and took his time licking the rough stuff. It felt cozy in there. She got horny. She licked his dick a little, then she put it in.

"Your vagina is extra warm," Boner said.

"Is it?"

"Yeah. I've only been with a few other girls. But their vaginas weren't nearly as warm."

She leaned forward and kissed him.

"Move it around, like you're mixing dough."

"Like this?"

She moaned.

"Nice. Now fuck me."

"I thought I was."

"I mean hump it. Hard."

He pushed it in as hard as he could. He gave nice long thrusts.

"This is really good exercise," he said.

Clitty laughed. "I know."

He kept humping.

Clitty noticed he was getting lightheaded. She got him on his back and rode. The head of his dick touched some deep parts. Her eyes widened. She moved her waist back and forth, quickly.

"It tickles!" he yelled.

He grabbed her by her waist and picked her up. He put her on the bed. She saw pussy grime on his dick. She grabbed it, put it in her mouth and sucked the slime off it.

Boner became dizzy.

She stopped sucking.

He put it back in. Gave it to her normal style.

"I think I need to come," he said.

"It's okay."

He pulled out and squirted on his own belly, and then passed out.

45

Clitty had another appointment so he couldn't stay. He napped with her for an hour or so, gave her the money he owed her, then left.

He felt better. He headed to a bar called The Chart Room. He drank alone for a bit, played the slot machines. He'd never had much luck with slot machines, but they reminded him of video games. He wished they could have arcade games in the bar.

Jake came in. Boner was happy to see the psycho. Boner got him a drink and then another.

The bar filled up.

They kept close. Jake smelled like Old Spice.

They talked about movies and women. Boner told him about his day with Clitty.

"My dick got so gooey," he said.

"I could tell that she had a gooey vagina," Jake said. "It's a sign of great vitality. She will most likely live for a long time."

Boner didn't understand what he was talking about. And he didn't care.

Some men were giving Jake a nasty look. He and Boner tried to ignore them, but things got tense. The two paid their tab and left for another bar.

The men followed them outside. There were two of them. One was short and stocky and especially irritable. His buddy was gangly and had a bad complexion.

"You need to stop harassing my sister," the short one said.

"Who?" Jake asked.

"You know, Maggie. You've been writing her all sorts of creepy letters. You fucking sick fuck. She's only sixteen."

"Fuck you," Boner said. "Stop being mean to my friend!"

"You nerds looking to get hurt?"

"No, we're looking to kick your ass. We know Kung Fu," Boner said. "Jake-style Kung Fu."

The two men laughed.

Boner ran at Zit Face. He jumped up and head butted the kid in the mouth. The tall guy went down.

Boner had one of Zit Face's teeth lodged in his forehead. He picked it out, looking at it in his hand.

"Wow. Intense," he said.

The ugly bulldog-looking one was about to charge, but Jake jumped on his back, landing his foot behind his knee, knocking him to the ground. He punched the big guy in his head. Hard. His knuckles burst open. Blood poured. Jake showed no pain.

Boner grabbed the man by his curly hair and punched his face a bunch of times, then slammed it into the bumper of a Dodge Caravan. He let the guy slump into a puddle of his own toothy blood.

"You okay?" he asked Jake.

Jake nodded.

A few more guys came out of the bar. They saw the two men bloody and groaning in the cement.

"What the fuck happened here?" one of them yelled.

They all went after Jake and Boner.

A dude with a ponytail threw a punch at Boner. Boner ducked and kicked the guy's ankle, breaking it. The guy fell into the fetal position, weeping and screaming.

A fat bearded fisherman punched Jake in the gut. Jake keeled over, then fell on his back, and kicked the man in his dick and nut sack with both feet. Fat Man bent over. Jake jumped to his feet. He grabbed Fat Man's hair and kneed him in the face, breaking his jaw and knocking him out. He pushed him on top of Ponytail.

The last man was about Boner's age. He had a shaved head and wore a wife beater. He looked freaked out. Jake and Boner looked at each other, nodded. The two buddies ran up and jump kicked the kid simultaneously. He fell to the ground. Boner and Jake continued kicking him until he was mashed up and unconscious.

46

Jake and Boner looked at the moaning, bleeding bodies. Boner smiled. He gave Jake a bear hug, lifting him up and shaking him. Jake laughed.

"That was awesome!" Boner yelled.

The bartender came out. She was crying.

"I'm calling the cops!" she yelled.

Boner put Jake down and they ran to the Honda.

"What happened to your minivan?" Jake asked.

"I had to sell it."

"Really? I'm sorry, man."

Boner's eyes became moist and withdrawn. He felt sad, but he also felt durable. It was important to feel durable, he decided.

He drove them through town, past the old Grimy Diner and the gas station where The Doctor worked. He drove over the bridge that went over the creek. He looped around the traffic circle and up Florence Avenue, then up West Lexington. His Grandma's house was up there. Some relatives had cleaned it out. There was a FOR SALE sign in the yard. Boner drove over the sign. He started doing donuts in the lawn. His tires made muddy circles in the grass. Jake looked scared but happy.

"This is fun. Very liberating!" he yelled.

Boner laughed.

He continued spinning around, tearing up the earth.

Justin Grimbol moves around a lot. He also writes books, touches butts and watches a lot of sappy movies.

Other Grindhouse Press Titles

#666__*Satanic Summer* by Andersen Prunty

#025__*Ghost Chant* by Gina Ranalli

#024__*Hearers of the Constant Hum* by William Pauley III

#023__*Hell's Waiting Room* by C.V. Hunt

#022__*Creep House: Horror Stories* by Andersen Prunty

#021__*Other People's Shit* by C.V. Hunt

#020__*The Party Lords* by Justin Grimbol

#019__*Sociopaths In Love* by Andersen Prunty

#018__*The Last Porno Theater* by Nick Cato

#017__*Zombieville* by C.V. Hunt

#016__*Samurai Vs. Robo-Dick* by Steve Lowe

#015__*The Warm Glow of Happy Homes* by Andersen Prunty

#014__*How To Kill Yourself* by C.V. Hunt

#013__*Bury the Children in the Yard: Horror Stories* by Andersen Prunty

#012 __*Return to Devil Town (Vampires in Devil Town Book Three)* by Wayne Hixon

#011__*Pray You Die Alone: Horror Stories* by Andersen Prunty

#010__*King of the Perverts* by Steve Lowe

#009__*Sunruined: Horror Stories* by Andersen Prunty

#008__*Bright Black Moon: Vampires in Devil Town Book Two* by Wayne Hixon

#007__*Hi I'm a Social Disease: Horror Stories* by Andersen Prunty

#006__*A Life On Fire* by Chris Bowsman

#005__*The Sorrow King* by Andersen Prunty

#004__*The Brothers Crunk* by William Pauley III

#003__*The Horribles* by Nathaniel Lambert

#002__*Vampires in Devil Town* by Wayne Hixon

#001__*House of Fallen Trees* by Gina Ranalli

#000__*Morning is Dead* by Andersen Prunty

www.ingramcontent.com/pod-product-compliance
Lightning Source LLC
Chambersburg PA
CBHW061453210726
48287CB00007B/2496